A Note to Parents

DK READERS is a compelling programme for beginning readers,
designe_   _   _
Maure_
years t_   _a_   _ol_
consulta_

Beautiful illustrations and superb full-colour photographs
combine with engaging, easy-to-read stories and informational
texts to offer a fresh approach to each subject in the series. Each
DK READER is guaranteed to capture a child's interest while
developing his or her reading skills, general knowledge and love
of reading.

The five levels of DK READERS are aimed at different reading
abilities, enabling you to choose the books that are exactly right
for your child:

> **Pre-level 1**: Learning to read
>
> **Level 1**: Beginning to read
>
> **Level 2**: Beginning to read alone
>
> **Level 3**: Reading alone
>
> **Level 4**: Proficient readers

The 'normal' age at which a child begins
to read can be anywhere from three to
eight years old. Adult participation through
the lower levels is very helpful for providing
encouragement, discussing storylines
and sounding out unfamiliar words.

No matter which level you select, you can
be sure that you are helping your child
to read, then read

LONDON, NEW YORK,
MELBOURNE, MUNICH and DELHI

For Dorling Kindersley
Project Editor Heather Scott
Designer Owen Bennett
Senior Designer Ron Stobbart
Art Director Lisa Lanzarini
Publishing Manager Simon Beecroft
Category Publisher Alex Allan
Production Controller Jen Lockwood
Production Editor Siu Chan

For Lucasfilm
Executive Editor Jonathan W. Rinzler
Art Director Troy Alders
Keeper of the Holocron Leland Chee
Director of Publishing Carol Roeder

Reading Consultant
Maureen Fernandes

First published in the Great Britain in 2009 by
Dorling Kindersley Limited
80 Strand, London, WC2R 0RL

6 8 10 9 7 5
SD410 – 10/08

A CIP catlogue record for this book
is available from the British Library

Published inthe USA by DK Publishing.

ISBN: 978-1-40533-860-8

Colour reproduction by MDP
Printed and bound by L-Rex, China

Discover more
www.dk.com
www.starwars.com

DK READERS

BEGINNING 1 TO READ

STAR WARS

LUKE SKYWALKER'S
AMAZING STORY

Written by Simon Beecroft

DK

This is Luke.

He dreams of having adventures.

He lives on a far away planet with his aunt and uncle.

His aunt and uncle are called...

Aunt Beru and Uncle Owen.

Uncle Owen is a farmer.

He buys two droids to help him on his farm.

The droids are called...

C-3PO and R2-D2.

R2-D2 has a secret message for a strange old man who lives nearby.

Luke watches the message.

The old man is called...

Obi-Wan Kenobi.

Obi-Wan Kenobi is a Jedi. He knew Luke's father.

Luke has never met his father.

Luke's father is called...

Anakin Skywalker.

Anakin Skywalker was once a
Jedi, like Obi-Wan Kenobi.

But Anakin turned to the
dark side of the Force.

Then he became
known as...

Darth Vader.

Darth Vader wants to rule
the galaxy.

Some people want to stop him.

They are called Rebels.

Darth Vader has captured the
leader of the Rebels.

She is called...

Princess Leia.

Princess Leia put the message
inside R2-D2 for Obi-Wan Kenobi.
She needs Obi-Wan's help.

Obi-Wan takes Luke to meet
two pilots.

The pilots are called...

Han Solo and Chewbacca.

They have a fast spaceship.
Obi-Wan asks Han Solo if he will
fly them into space.

Han Solo says he will. So...

Luke, Obi-Wan, Han Solo, Chewbacca, C-3PO and R2-D2 all fly in the fast spaceship to a big space station called the Death Star.

Some soldiers try
to capture them.
The soldiers
are called...

Stormtroopers.

They are Darth Vader's soldiers.
Luke, Han and Chewbacca fight
the Stormtroopers.

They rescue Princess Leia.
They take Leia to...

The Rebels.

The Rebels attack the Death Star in their spaceships.

Luke blows up the Death Star with a very lucky shot.

Later Luke visits...

Yoda.

Yoda is a Jedi. He lives in a swamp.

Yoda trains Luke to be a Jedi.
Luke realises it is time to meet...

His father, Darth Vader.

Darth Vader wants Luke to
become bad,
like him.

In the end, Luke
helps Darth
Vader become
good again.

Darth Vader
turns back into...

Anakin Skywalker, Luke's real father.

Luke takes off Darth Vader's helmet. Luke looks at his father's face.

He is happy to see his father at last.

Quiz!

1. Who is Luke's father?

2. What is this droid's name?

3. Who is this?

4. Who teaches Luke to be a Jedi?

Answers: 1. Anakin Skywalker, 2. C-3PO, 3. Princess Leia, 4. Yoda